GW00870286

Fiesta Cane

Fiesta Cane

A Blind Mama's Gift

Natalie Watkins

Indy Pub

Editing, print layout, e–book conversion,
and cover design by DLD Books
Editing and Self–Publishing Services

DLD Books

www.dldbooks.com

Illustrations by Bianca Silva

ISBN: 978-1-0880-8784-8

Introduction

Fiesta has been celebrated in San Antonio for many years to honor the heroes of the Alamo. Today children have fun going to parties and parades. It is a festive time with family, friends, and food.

Today was the day of the big fiesta.

Adriana was worried.

April

She was worried at breakfast.

She was worried on the big yellow bus.

She was worried at the library.

She was even worried at lunch.

Alex was scared when he put his shoes on.

He was scared on his walk to school.

He was scared when he put away his backpack.

And he was scared when he ate his lunch.

At recess, Alex and Adriana hid behind the same tree.

"What's wrong?" Alex asked.

"I'm worried Mama will get made fun of at the fiesta because she's blind and uses a cane. Why are *you* hiding here?"

HA
HA HA

“I’m scared I’ll get bullied at the fiesta because my face looks different,” Alex said.

“Let’s be braver!” Adriana replied.

“Braver!” Alex repeated.

“How do we do that?” Alex asked.

“I know! We don’t hide,” Adriana said.

“We don’t hide!” Alex repeated.

They came out from behind the tree.

"Now what?" Adriana asked.

"I know! We can make party canes for the fiesta! That way your mama won't be the only person with a cane at the fiesta!" Alex said.

Adriana picked up branches from the ground.

CRACK!

Together they decorated them with paint, glitter, and ribbons inside the classroom.

The other kids saw what they were doing.

Alex showed them how to find branches. They all rushed and decorated their canes.

TAP. TAP. TAP. Adriana heard Mama come down the hall. Mama used her cane to feel her way around.

Tap
Tap
Tap

"You get a super surprise!" Alex said to Mama.

“We made fiesta canes!” Adriana said.

"The whole class has canes like yours. They're bright branches with glitter and ribbons."

Alex felt brave.

Adriana felt brave.

The whole class wanted to go to the fiesta.

Viva la fiesta!

La Fiesta

About the Author

Natalie Watkins lives in South Texas and loves weaving words and ideas. Inspired by the potential of the written word to engender empathy, she writes children's literature, poetry, creative nonfiction, and blog posts.

A proud member of the blind and visually impaired community, she provides support to those new to vision loss. In addition, she is on the board of a nonprofit that serves the blind and visually impaired.

Natalie appreciates the opportunity to share her work with others and has been published in the *San Antonio Express–News* and the *Houston Chronicle*. She has placed in poetry contests sponsored by the National Federation of the Blind and the organization Writing Works Wonders. She also enjoys being on panels at book festivals and doing readings of her work.

A wife and the mother of two teens, she treasures time spent with family and friends.

January 2023

Email: natalie.watkins107@gmail.com
Website: https://www.dldbooks.com/nataliewatkins/

Ingram Content Group UK Ltd.
Milton Keynes UK
UKHW050741280323
419269UK00002B/10

9781088087848